PAUL
and his
FRIENDS

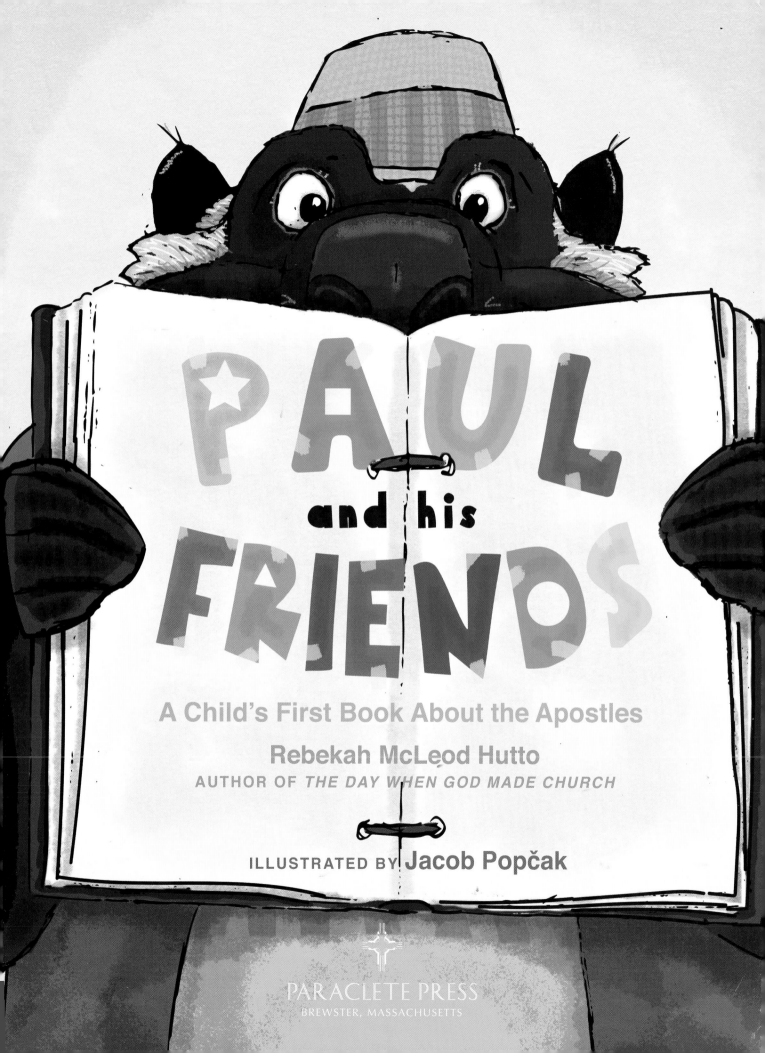

PAUL
and his
FRIENDS

A Child's First Book About the Apostles

Rebekah McLeod Hutto

AUTHOR OF *THE DAY WHEN GOD MADE CHURCH*

ILLUSTRATED BY **Jacob Popčak**

PARACLETE PRESS
BREWSTER, MASSACHUSETTS

2018 First Printing

Paul and His Friends: A Child's First Book About the Apostles

Text copyright © 2018 Rebekah McLeod Hutto
Illustrations copyright © 2018 Jacob Harrison Popčak

ISBN 978-1-61261-945-3

The Paraclete Press name and logo (dove on cross) are trademarks of Paraclete Press, Inc.

Library of Congress Cataloging-in-Publication:

Names: Hutto, Rebekah McLeod, author.
Title: Paul and his friends : a child's first book about the apostles /
  Rebekah McLeod Hutto, author of The Day When God Made
Church ; illustrated
  by Jacob Popcak.
Description: Brewster, MA : Paraclete Press, Inc., 2018.
Identifiers: LCCN 2018024110 | ISBN 9781612619453 (trade paper)
Subjects: LCSH: Paul, the Apostle, Saint--Juvenile literature. | Paul,
the Apostle, Saint--Friends and associates--Juvenile literature.
Classification: LCC BS2506.5 .H88 2018 | DDC 225.92/2--dc23
LC record available at https://lccn.loc.gov/2018024110

10 9 8 7 6 5 4 3 2 1

Published by Paraclete Press
Brewster, Massachusetts
www.paracletepress.com

Printed in United States of America

To my best friend and favorite editor,
my beloved husband B.J.
Thank you for your encouragement
and support.
Your friendship is one of the
greatest gifts of my life,
and I dedicate this book to you.
—RMH

To Mike, for the introduction,
To Kaiser Gavin, for the inspiration,
And to God and my family for
everything else.
—JP

My name is Paul. I lived a long time ago. I was a friend of Jesus and one of the Apostles. I helped people all over the world learn about Jesus's love.

Jesus met me one day on the road and spoke to me in a blinding light.[1] On that day my life was changed forever, and I couldn't wait to tell others.

I traveled all over the world, meeting new people, sharing stories of Jesus. I helped teach people how to love like Jesus, and I wrote letters to them when they had questions. I met many new people who helped me all along the way. From the beginning of my journey, I was never alone.

First, there was my friend Ananias who helped me when I needed food and rest.[2] He called me "Brother," and he prayed for me. He put his hands around me and made me feel less afraid. He reminded me that I wasn't alone.

Just like Ananias, other friends took care of me throughout my ministry. I'd love for you to meet them. Would you like to hear their stories?

This is my friend Barnabas. I met him soon after I became a follower of Jesus.[3] Barnabas gave me courage and supported me when I was alone.

He was brave and encouraged many others to follow Jesus.[4] He and I traveled together to share Jesus's love. Barnabas was a good friend: kind, a wonderful teacher.

This is my friend Silas. Like Barnabas, he also traveled with me, preaching and teaching. Sometimes our preaching and teaching about Jesus made other people mad. Once, in Philippi, we were even arrested and thrown in jail.[5]

But Silas stayed with me, and we sang and prayed together.

When God freed us from our jail cell, we rejoiced. This miracle helped encourage others to believe in Jesus too. Many people took care of us and fed us in their homes.

This is my friend Lydia. She was a leader among her friends in Philippi.[6] She sold expensive purple cloth, and many people respected her.

I met her one day while she was praying with other women by the river. Lydia was kind to my friends and me and offered us a place to stay. She fed us, gave us a place to rest, and shared what she had with us.

These are my friends Priscilla and Aquila, a married couple who were leaders in their church.[7] Without these friends, I would have felt alone and lost in the city of Corinth.

As Lydia did, Priscilla and Aquila gave me a place to stay and took care of me when I traveled. Both Priscilla and Aquila were teachers who helped share stories of Jesus.

This is Timothy, one of my closest friends during my ministry.[8] Timothy's faith in God was strong, thanks to his grandmother Lois, and his mother, Eunice.[9] We traveled a lot together, along with our friend Luke, who was a doctor.

Timothy stayed with me even when my travels became dangerous. I trusted Timothy, and his friendship was very special to me.

This is my friend Phoebe. She was a trusted follower of Jesus, and I called her "Sister."[10] Like Lydia, she was a leader in her church.

Phoebe supported my ministry and helped me deliver a letter to followers of Jesus who lived in Rome. Phoebe was a deacon in her church—someone chosen to lead and care for others.

This is Philemon, one of my friends who helped lead a church in Colossae.[11]

Sometimes friends have to help one another do the right thing. One time, I wrote to Philemon to help him make a good decision. We both knew a man named Onesimus, and he and Philemon had not been friends for a long time. This made me very sad, so I encouraged Philemon to forgive Onesimus. In my letter, I told Philemon to welcome Onesimus home and love him as a brother.

Speaking of forgiveness, I haven't always been a good friend to others. For example, I once knew a man named Stephen. He was a great leader in the church, reminding everyone to care for their neighbors. Stephen was killed by people who listened to the mean things I used to say about Jesus before I knew Jesus myself.

Sometimes friends make mistakes, and we all need God's help to make better choices.

When Jesus was with his disciples he told them he was their friend.[12] He said he was like a vine and they were like branches, connected to him by love.

Jesus wants us to love others just as he loves us. Because we are his friends, Jesus teaches us how to be a good friend to everyone we meet.

And although it may be a difficult thing to do, Jesus also tells us to love our enemies just as we love our friends. Even when people are not kind, even when they hurt us—we are called to love them as Jesus loves them. Just as Jesus loves us.

All love comes from God. When we love others, even our enemies, we teach others about God's love.

The day the church began, Jesus's followers became each other's friends. They made friends with people from different nations who spoke different languages.

They shared their food and homes with each other.[13] As good friends, they made sure to take care of one another.

Friends celebrate with us when we're happy.
Friends cheer us up when we're sad.
Friends forgive us when we make mistakes.
Friends give us courage when we're afraid.
Friends remind us we're never alone.

One of God's greatest gifts is a friend.
We should treasure our friends, the ones who love us and care for us.

I, Paul, was blessed to have many friends, and I want to be your friend too.
You are never alone.
God is always with you, even when you are sad and afraid.

You are always loved. God loves you. And remember that you are always forgiven, especially when you make mistakes. Jesus will always be your friend.

23

Scripture references

1   Acts 9
2   Acts 9:17–19
3   Acts 9:27
4   Acts 11:23–24
5   Acts 16:16–34
6   Acts 16:14–16, 40
7   Acts 18:1–3, 26
8   Philippians 2:19–24
9   2 Timothy 1:5
10   Romans 16:1–2
11   Philemon
12   John 15:1–17
13   Acts 2:44–46

Sources for the animal characters in this book:

Paul and his friends were real people, but in this book, they are re-imagined as animals from the real Paul's part of the world. Learn more about them below!

1. Paul is depicted as a honey badger. Honey badgers can be found throughout the Holy Land. Although they look cuddly, they are also known for their toughness, just like Paul.

2. Barnabas is a crocodile. Barnabas may be friendly, but crocodiles are also very fierce. They are mentioned many times throughout the Bible.

3. Silas is a hyena. Hyenas are known for their bark, which sounds a lot like laughing. Silas is known for the joyful spirit he kept, even while in prison.

4. Lydia is a sheep. Sheep can be found everywhere throughout the Holy Land, where their wool is used to make cloth. Lydia is famous for making purple cloth, which was very beautiful.

5. Priscilla and Aquila are depicted as elephants. Elephants are known for being strong, wise, and noble, just like Priscilla and Aquila.

6. Timothy is a Thomson's gazelle, a very common kind of gazelle found in East Africa. Gazelles are very shy, just like Timothy. But even when times got tough, Timothy did his best to stay brave.

7. Phoebe is a camel. Camels are also common in the Holy Land. They are famous for being able to travel many miles, just as the disciples of Christ had to do in order to spread the word of God.

8. Saint Stephen is a caracal, a type of wild cat native to the Holy Land. The name "Stephen" comes from the Greek title "Stephanos," which means "wreath" or "crown." Some people think the black markings on a caracal's head look like a crown.

9. In this book, Jesus is depicted as a lion. Jesus is sometimes called "the Lion of Judah" in the Bible, because lions are often seen as "kings" and because they fiercely protect those they love, just like Jesus.

10. There were many followers of Jesus present at Pentecost. Among the figures in our book, notice these three friends. Depending on what translation of the Bible you read, the same animal is translated as either a wild ox, a rhino, or a unicorn. What is the right translation? The answer doesn't matter much to these friends.

—Jacob Popčak

Use this page to draw some of your friends.

Use this page to draw some of your friends.

About Paraclete Press

As the publishing arm of the Community of Jesus, Paraclete Press presents a full expression of Christian belief and practice—from Catholic to Evangelical, from Protestant to Orthodox, reflecting the ecumenical charism of the Community and its dedication to sacred music, the fine arts, and the written word. We publish books, recordings, sheet music, and video/DVDs that nourish the vibrant life of the church and its people.

What We Are Doing

Books

PARACLETE PRESS BOOKS show the richness and depth of what it means to be Christian. While Benedictine spirituality is at the heart of who we are and all that we do, our books reflect the Christian experience across many cultures, time periods, and houses of worship.

We have many series, including Paraclete Essentials; Paraclete Fiction; Paraclete Poetry; Paraclete Giants; and for children and adults, *All God's Creatures*, books about animals and faith; and *San Damiano Books*, focusing on Franciscan spirituality. Others include *Voices from the Monastery* (men and women monastics writing about living a spiritual life today), *Active Prayer*, and new for young readers: *The Pope's Cat*. We also specialize in gift books for children on the occasions of Baptism and First Communion, as well as other important times in a child's life, and books that bring creativity and liveliness to any adult spiritual life.

The MOUNT TABOR BOOKS series focuses on the arts and literature as well as liturgical worship and spirituality; it was created in conjunction with the Mount Tabor Ecumenical Centre for Art and Spirituality in Barga, Italy.

Music

The PARACLETE RECORDINGS label represents the internationally acclaimed choir *Gloriæ Dei Cantores*, the *Gloriæ Dei Cantores Schola*, and the other instrumental artists of the Arts Empowering Life Foundation.

Paraclete Press is the exclusive North American distributor for the Gregorian chant recordings from St. Peter's Abbey in Solesmes, France. Paraclete also carries all of the Solesmes chant publications for Mass and the Divine Office, as well as their academic research publications.

In addition, PARACLETE PRESS SHEET MUSIC publishes the work of today's finest composers of sacred choral music, annually reviewing over 1,000 works and releasing between 40 and 60 works for both choir and organ.

Video

Our video/DVDs offer spiritual help, healing, and biblical guidance for a broad range of life issues including grief and loss, marriage, forgiveness, facing death, understanding suicide, bullying, addictions, Alzheimer's, and Christian formation.

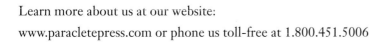

Learn more about us at our website:
www.paracletepress.com or phone us toll-free at 1.800.451.5006

SCAN TO READ MORE

You might also like to read....

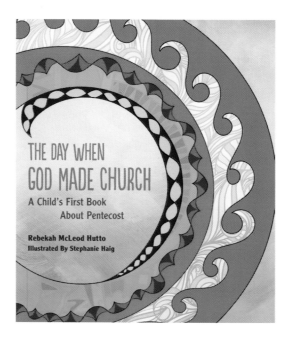

The Day When God Made Church
A Child's Book About Pentecost

Rebekah McLeod Hutto
Illustrated by Stephanie Haig

$15.99 Paperback | ISBN 978-1-61261-564-6

Learn to celebrate Pentecost—the Church's birthday!

Do you know the story of Pentecost? This book will teach you all about the sights, the sounds, and the people that began the community of the Church. Read it together, and you and your parents, your teachers, and even your minister will discover the coming of the Holy Spirit in exciting new ways!

"Readers and listeners of all ages will discover much to stimulate their understanding of Pentecost through this theologically grounded book."

—MELANIE C. GORDON,
Director of Ministry with Children, Discipleship Ministries of the UMC

Available at bookstores.
Paraclete Press | 1-800-451-5006
www.paracletepress.com